Published originally under the title:
Die Perle by Helme Heine
by Gertraud Middelhauve Verlag, Köln
Copyright © 1984 by Gertraud Middelhauve Verlag, Köln
English translation copyright © 1985 by J. M. Dent & Sons Ltd., London
All rights reserved
Library of Congress catalog card number: 84-72404
ISBN 0-689-50321-0
Printed in Germany
First American Edition

The Pearl

Helme Heine

A MARGARET K. McELDERRY BOOK

Atheneum   1985   New York

The little boat drifted slowly away but Beaver did not
notice it. He could think of nothing but the shell he had
found while playing in the lake.

He looked at it from every angle, sniffing it thoroughly.
There was no doubt about it: it was a freshwater
pearl mussel.

Beaver had found a treasure — or at least a treasure-
chest. Not for one moment did he doubt that there was a
pearl inside the mussel. Why else would it be called a
pearl mussel? Overcome with happiness, Beaver hugged
the mussel to his heart, closed his eyes and
began to dream. . .

He dreamed that his friends were looking at him in astonishment. "Beaver has found the greatest treasure in the forest," they said to themselves, and they were filled with envy.

When they asked where the pearl had come from, Beaver
stammered: "From the forest. Under a toadstool. A long
way from here. A very long way."

His friends did not believe him. "Pearls are found in
mussels in the lake," they said. "Not in the forest."
Leaving him, they began to search the shallow waters
near the shore.

"This is my lake!" screamed Beaver. "I built the dam.
The mussels are mine!"

At first none of his friends paid the slightest attention to him. But finally the bear — in a furious temper — growled: "And what did you use to build your dam? You used trees. And they came from our forest. Therefore, the lake and all the mussels we find are ours."

There was nothing Beaver could do but watch helplessly while more and more animals joined in the treasure hunt.

Many of the animals could not swim or even paddle.
They destroyed Beaver's dam so all the water ran out.
Then they, too, searched frantically for mussels.

Up to their knees in sand and mud, the treasure hunters
squabbled over every mussel, hurling insults and
mud at each other.

As darkness fell, the treasure hunters built a huge bonfire.

They were afraid that owls and bats would steal their
mussels. Exhausted though they were, they kept
watch all night.

Suddenly, a gust of wind showered the forest with sparks
and flames from the bonfire. Beaver's house was soon
ablaze — and there was no water in the lake with which
to fight the fire. It destroyed everything, even Beaver
and the pearl . . .

. . . Beaver awoke terrified from his horrible dream.
While he thought about it he looked at the mussel he had
not yet opened.

Picking it up, he hurled the mussel as far as he could
into the lake.

It skimmed the surface, bouncing seven times before it sank, something he had never managed to do before.

Then, happy once more, Beaver plunged into the water and swam after his little boat. It had nearly reached the other side of the lake where all his friends were waiting for him to come and play.